5.00

The Ra

Also by Rienzi Crusz

Flesh and Thorn
Elephant and Ice
Singing against the Wind
A Time for Loving (TSAR book)
Still Close to the Raven (TSAR book)

The Rain Doesn't Know Me Anymore

Poems

by

Rienzi Crusz

TSAR
Toronto
1992

The publishers acknowledge generous assistance
from the Ontario Arts Council and the Canada Council.
© 1992 Rienzi Crusz
Except for purposes of review, no part of this book may be
reproduced in any form without prior permission of the publisher.

ISBN 0-920661-26-2

TSAR Publications
P.O. Box 6996, Station A
Toronto, M5W 1X7 Canada

Cover design: Virgil Burnett

For

the Beautiful Vikings

Deena and Jens

Acknowledgements

Some of these poems first appeared in the following journals: *Quarry; Fiddlehead; Descant; Canadian Literature; The Toronto South Asian Review; Grail; Kunapipi; Currents; The New Quarterly.*

I thank the Multiculturalism Sector, Department of the Secretary of State, for its financial assistance in writing this book; the Ontario Arts Council for various grants; and the University of Waterloo for sabbatical leave of absence.

Life can only be understood backwards;
but it must be lived forwards.
       SOREN KIERKEGAARD

Contents

1
bouquet to my colonial masters 2
the geography of voice 3
why I can talk of the angelic qualities of the raven 4
my son 5
the rain doesn't know me any more 6
the weather reporters 7
home 8
distant rain 10
civilization 11
the midnight hour / before citizenship 13
O Canada 14

2
eyeline 18
learning the language 19
scars 21
the art of self-deception 22
for the man who nailed a dried Maple leaf outside his office door 23
the painter 25
masks 27
mermaid 28
all I ask is my life 29
reincarnation 30
some thoughts on the Indian Rope Trick 31
elegy for the perfect man 32
legend of the ice-hole child 34
breaking the silence 36
the man who didn't jump from the Golden Gate Bridge 37
the Bilian Tree 38
karma 39

3
return of the fishermen 42
he who talks to the raven 43
waif 45

the outlaw and the orchid 46
Kukul Charlie 47

4
the accepted one 50
heart of the matter 51
"Yes, in our Father's House there are many rooms" 52

5
how an old poet beat loneliness to death 56
poetics 57
letter of thanks to my first creative writing teacher 58
the separate one 60

6
domestic history 62
love poem for Anne #2 64
genetics 65
elegy for an elder brother 66
the perfect hobbyist 67
for Michael dancing with his hands on his head 68
love poem for Anne #3 69
leaving–Michael style 70
connections of a passionate sort 72
a time for epitaphs 73
sunday morning 76

1

only by dying
do we learn the true rhythms
of the heart, by crying,
how to laugh from the belly

bouquet to my colonial masters

Gauguin's woman under another sun
raped. How silence spilled
from an abattoir of tongues.

And you still show me
your polished bannisters,
your country estates,
green, columned and groomed.

How your freighters coughed black,
then guffawed and left heavy
with coconut and tea,
cardamom, cinnamon and ivory,
the sandalwood artifacts
still leaking their exotic perfume
from their dark holds.

And through it all
I heard the Englishman's siesta snore,
the civilized cooing
of civilized men
gulping their velvet whiskies,
as brown waiters bent and bowed
to the evening noise of their masters.

So what was left to keep?
Shakespeare!
a tongue to speak with,
some words to remember.
Today,
we are all poets
for having suffered the chains,
for having learnt the language.

the geography of voice

My lady, so close to me
for so long,
your pale mouth spills decibels
high and low about my ears,
voices that divide like geography
from a cool cutting bitch's tone,
to mongrel dialect,
epiphanies and laughter.

In the cold cotton-white land
where your hibiscus heart
freezes to its roots,
you talk from the head, cold
and final as winter's argument.

Travelling south, out of town,
the sun flavouring you like gravy,
you turn ethnic, a voice
dragging sun tones, a vocabulary
much like your Sri Lankan grandmother's.

Back to your cradled beginnings
where you heard the elephant
challenge the inconsistent moon,
pariah dogs barking
at nothing but hot air, children
crying "sadhu, sadhu" on their way
to the Temple,
you are belly laughter, epiphanic voice
drumming the limbs of the Kandyan dancer.

why I can talk of the angelic qualities of the raven

Let's talk colours.
Start with BLACK,
that true hallmark of the sun.
What else
is the eye of the hurricane, the colour
of magic night?
Is the Geisha, Geisha
without her black crown
against porcelain skin?
If the raven talks, listen.
It's God in winged disguise.

What's coloured
(blue, cinnabar, turquoise)
always throbs like a lover's heart.
The bougainvillea
under a Trinidad sun
holds the magic of metaphors,
sets off the quality
of our sunsets, our batik effusions,
our Gauguins, our murders.

As for WHITE,
read the instructions carefully:
FRAGILE   HANDLE WITH CARE   THIS SIDE UP
May be too precious
for ordinary use, extraordinary pain;
the angelic colour
often overwhelms,
is much like strobe glare
over desert sands.

And what about BROWN
or its variants:
olive, beige, sunburnt yellow?

they hardly preach, intrude,
refuse to wilt under the sun
and yet, could be
as lush and vibrant
as a Kandyan maid.

No; colour has nothing to do with it.
What you imagine
is all that matters.
The rest is too real to be true.
The apple was only cinema,
so was the serpent, the woman.
What was real
was Original Sin.
Adam slapping God
on his cosmic ears.

my son

the blood I spilled for you
was real.
For twenty years I waited
at the City gates
for darkness to fall, for stars
to guide my immigrant feet.
Only by dying
do we learn the true rhythms
of the heart, by crying,
how to laugh from the belly.

the rain doesn't know me any more

I shape forgotten metaphor:
curved tusks, howdah and mahout;
splash the Bird of Paradise
against a cemetery of cars,
seek the root in cabook earth,
the dream   that meandered, got lost
in a theatre of blood.

I who held the palm tree's silhouette
against the going sun, a woman,
a child   long enough
to divide a continent,
have new revelations:
I have circled the sun.
The white marshmallow land
is now mine, conquered,
cussed upon, loved.

Look at this dreaming face,
these new muscles, tempered bones,
black eyes   blue
with a new landscape,
legs dancing the white slopes
like a dervish.
Against paddy bird havocking in tall grass,
blue jay raucous, cardinals
the colour of blood.
For the homecoming catamaran,
747 screaming,
wounding the night like a spear.

The monsoon rain
doesn't know me any more.
I'm now snowbank child, bundled,
with snot under my nose,

snowflake magic in both hands.
Once, rice and curry, passion juice,
now, hot dogs and fries,
Black Forest Ham on Rye.

So what's the essential story?
Nothing　　but a journey done,
a horizon that never stands still.

the weather reporters

I can see you now, you
    in your thick blue snowsuit
    fluffing up the snowman,
    drip under your nose, eyes watering,
    streaking your pink cheeks.
    Your mother hardly worries,
    keeps to her regular SOAPS, knowing
    how you thrive in cold snow.

My feet are bare,
    my brown skin always turns
    like a compass to the sun.
    I'm best round 80 degrees
    in the shade.
    Civilization here dresses only
    in short pants and gauze banian
    for play.
    Hands you a cricket bat.
    I'm well behind the ball,
    thrash my brother's googly
    clear over the fence.

If you hear me talk
    you'll perhaps hear
    some separate sounds,

      something like monsoon tantrums,
      cry of peacock, lagoon
      breathing at evening,
      the cockney chatter of crow.
      If you think you won't understand,
      you will. Shakespeare still walks
      the ramparts of my tongue
      like Hamlet's ghost.

So what happens to language
      when the mercury plunges
      one fall afternoon
      and your weather report
      turns passionate!

O my blond snowsuited boy
      here's an effusion for an effusion,
      the other language from somewhere
      directly over the equator:
      It's cold, damn cold, and I need
      a few more degrees of civilization
      to come even close to declaring
      this day   wonderful!

home

This poem is
going nowhere,
or so it seems.
But it's going–
there's some pain in the left clavicle,
an arthritic tug somewhere
on the right knee,
but stride and motion are still in rhythm,
and the unknown road
will twist and turn

to somewhere.

So it goes, is going,
bright red knapsack on its back,
jeans and sneakers to match,
sun shades and granola bars
to nurse the eyes, the belly's
distant rumblings;
and the born-again flower child
will be at it once more,
loafing down the 90s road
to home. This poem

like some documentary
spinning out stories
of an immigrant sun-man
hitting the unknown trails:
from Colombo to Amsterdam,
Zurich, London, New York,
Toronto, then Waterloo
Waterloo, Waterloo.

Home is where
another man
is your brother's face
and any old lady sitting on a porch
with salmon-pink wool on her lap,
a grey cat on the ledge
is nobody
but your mother,

where the truth happens
like a prayer
in a small white room
where laughter tickles
the bed-head sunflowers,
and we fold our tired travelling eyes at last.

distant rain

Your exotic pot
of white rose hibiscus
has never known the virago caress
of a monsoon rain.
So memory for you, my son,
is without green history.

As glass and stone
have framed your dark eyes
and all you know
is that land that falls asleep
in soft white pyjamas,

I guess you can keep on
asking angrily:
Do you have to hang up your story
like a butcher's side of beef?
Why another poem?
Why roll the rock
from the mouth of the tomb,
what's there in shadows, dry bones,
memories?

I raise my tired eyes
from the poem
that seduced my night, a poem
still new, fierce and lamenting:
"The Rain Doesn't Know Me Any More"
        To remember, to remember
the raindrops
bigger than my childhood eyes,
those blue fists
fast and liquid as a therapist's,

how the good earth churned

its red dust bowl,
then burgeoned to batik profusion,
and the sky caught the colours below
like a memory.

civilization

Dollar-Daze, Days
at Zellers County Fair,
and the parking lot
like some African watering-hole,
gathers in its animals.

The way they spill out
of their polished automobile skins,
drooling with Dollar-Daze,
ham on rye, the second cup free.

Supermarket vertigo,
and like everybody else
I roam the gleaming jungle,
now nowhere near the centre (of reason)
nothing but my head full

of cut prices, secret desires
to squeeze the CHARMIN,
jaws tight
on the raw meat of civilization.

Soon, I'm no more the hunter
but the hunted
as shelves beckon, seduce
like women of the evening,

and I surrender
to HEAVENLY HASH, pig tails,
cocktail wieners, almost anything

that bears a price slash on its face.

O God, I now feel
like the plastic bauble
at two-for-a-dollar,
the 50% discount coat
hanging limp and old
on its rack,

am surging
with the hysterical women
for the shimmering polyester satin,
the Velours warm as blood,
watching how their eyes burn
like warring gods,
becoming
just another shape
on a sewing machine.

All this metaphor
for nothing
but food, clothing and shelter?

the midnight hour / before citizenship

Striving   up river
and the coiled currents chanting:
   Heaven is here but hard to find,
   Heaven is hard to find but here.

Where darkness must first fall
like concrete, and every star
go out silently like a thief,
and the night is thick
with fireflies without fire.

What you have now is a small hell
(on the way to heaven)
a job bloodied
on the eerie rhythms
of a midnight conveyor belt.

So, press on, even though all you seek
is a small wood frame house
with cheap vinyl floors,
a Taiwan telephone,
but voices, yes voices
thick as honey, a nationality,
a citizenship
whole and unhyphenated.

O Canada

Come. We must rest here.

The land may freeze
even as we admire her blonde hair,
buttock lines, but Union Gas
will safely toast the chilling air
for our brown skins.
Expect some darkness from this woman,
a broken heart may sometimes cry
on her porcelain breasts.

This could be the promised land.

Turn on the TV. You might hit
the Buffalo Evening News and learn
the true colour of death, or wait,
"Married With Children" might uncover
the art of winning
by playing the superb loser.

This could be the promised land.

Patience. The cold comes and the cold goes,
goes with the crocus.
Golden rod and sumach will then riot
for a season.
If you would rather have the white slopes,
rum in hot chocolate,
wait out the death of butterflies,
the carnival of falling leaves.
I'd take the green now,
sun and the Lazy-Boy,
let the blood summer at 70.

This could be the promised land.

I'd ask:
Where else
could we sing those other melodies,
hear the new accents, keep our gods,
our basmati rice ?
But then what happens to those
still in dark corners,
a pox on the colour of their skins,
new immigrants with stones in their mouths?

O Canada.

2

till he finds the absolute darkness
the perfect frame of light

eyeline

The Buddha's eyes
always downcast
in sweet repose.
Demons long gone,
a world without a world.

Some Roman head in stone,
or Rembrandt's man
keeps staring
as if another encounter
were about to begin
or was always there.

Or take this old Egyptian fruitseller,
this Pharaoh's head,
they wear their eyes with that look
that's beyond horizon,
beyond history.

I'm without eyeline,
my eyeballs the lizard's,
rolling on a strange axis
to catch each each spark of light,
each jumping shadow,
just before it stoops to drink.

learning the language

Looks as if
    the once warm fires of the womb,
    my mother's passionate lingo,
    father's reason, cold
    under the arches of the brain
    would no longer do. Spaces,

sights, reasons   outside
    teach another way to dance,
    reach the leaping fire, to die:
    So this alphabet
    is also the man unable to work his legs,
    whose hands shake with the palsy;
    is when a black guide-dog and white cane
    become eyes
    and this man's map
    is only in his head, a world seen
    through his ears.

Is about the woman
    that reeks with ESTEE LAUDER,
    takes my eyes to her tousled head,
    her ankles hot as castanets,
    then casts off my face as ethnic.
    Or the preacher
    hurling fire and brimstone,
    the love of God, my fellow-worshipper
    killing my brown skin and dark suit
    with only his silence   his eyes.

Is the language
    in the aquarium's hurricane moments
    when the goldfish suddenly go vertical
    with snouts greedy and mean
    in the green gravel,

    their camouflage
    a fluttering of three-pronged tails
    like silver-red butterflies.

Or take the cat
    (rehearsing for the evening hunt)
    fashioning angles out of air,
    then preaching the silent crouch,
    the loaded, concealed paw
    for the curtains that sway,
    betray their nervous Sheers.

How else can we learn
    this grammar of pain, these idioms
    of love, laughter and deceit,
    this vocabulary
    of people, places, events
    that intersect like geometry?
    And how can we fashion
    that brass and confident mouth
    that can say
    even when the house is on fire:

    everything is OK.

scars

Anonymity spreads no colour,
is theatre without passion, denouement;
is amoeba, blank space,
trivia to which history
has not spoken.

So, if you must draw blood,
plunge the knife deep
and let there be the spasm,
the orgasm of blood.

What of the cobra's cool underbelly,
the poison locked in its jaws?
The apple's historic wound,
teeth-marks that preach
of Adam's cosmic fault?
These deaths are but tame.

Only when the wound sings
in its blood,
the flesh pommelled, reshaped;
and there's another Christ on a cross,
and darkness falls in the Twelfth Hour
and a crucifixion is done,
a resurrection begun,

will we hear the cock crow,
learn how history turns
on some shapeless scars.

the art of self-deception

When in doubt
    we sometimes ruffle our hair
and stare long
    into bedroom mirrors.
The mirrors stare back
    with equal doubt.

One way to certainty, they say,
    is to confirm
the velvet flesh on our faces,
    the eyes in our sockets.
Is the hair turbulent or tame
    on our doubting heads?

But when we do
    our real skins reveal
the blush, mascara, PORCELANA,
    KLEIN'S OBSESSION magic,
and certainty wears the

made-up face of doubt.

for the man who nailed a dried Maple leaf outside his office door

for Gary Draper

You were the Chief,
I   the Indian.
You stewed in strategies,
I was given to understanding–

You could nail anything
(except, perhaps, Playboy's
centrefold)
on to your office door.
But your iconography of leaf,
that castrated image
of the magnificent King Maple
raised questions, a curtain
on the theatre of your mind.
Why a dead leaf? What of one
with the crimson blush
that was its summer face?

If it's timing,
I take it you discount
the here and now,
summer's brief effervescence,
go for history, memorabilia,
the hardness of stone;
of politics,
I read a sudden rush
of cold Canadian blood to your head,
almost hear you choking
on   O Canada !

If it's power,

it tells me of strange detours,
the idiosyncrasies of power.
So all my dissent
in aesthetics, art,
image or iconography
remains only a storm
in my closed mouth.

Knowing you, however,
I suspect reasons
of literary bias
against fish stories,
how you prefer winter's
cold and balming silence
to summer's brash dalliance,
the noise of its clapping audience.
There's always peace in death,
life is too often
the tiger by the tail.

And then maybe
it's the icon of the cross
all over again–
that cycle of death and resurrection,
a brown de-veined Maple leaf
crucified to your office door
only a signature
of your usual compassion,
your love.

the painter

Who, having grappled
with rust, vermilion,
a deep deep red,
settles on God
as an apricot sun.

Whose man
is a host of eagles soaring,
screaming, 747s cutting the night sky;
is a cemetery of souls
scratching their own epitaphs.

Whose hell
is love, gypsy and designing,
the exotic woman
with a Temple flower
in her black hair.

Whose heaven
is no more
than the silhouette
of a baby's cheek.

Whose love
is two paddy birds tumbling
in the tall grass,
feathers fluffed, fused
by an abetting sun.

Whose heart
throbs wildly
as his image begins to distil
from the fires of the sun,
the moods of the moon
flaunting and fading,

until he finds
the absolute darkness,
the perfect frame
Of light.

masks

The midnight sun
hovers like an angel
over this Northern City, Sundsvaal.
Its massive red eye
breaks the summer darkness
into a thousand shards of shimmer,
shapes a restless carnival crowd;
the sun is paying for the sins
of eternal winter,
those long killing snows.

Willie, my Casanova cat,
has made his last tryst
with his sand-coloured Ramona;
he runs his small bones
under a sand truck.
One remembers not the lump of fur
blotted in blood,
only the happy trips,
the sandy-haired girl in his green eyes.

My son, Michael, deftly uses his crayons
to draw yet another variation
of the "Boglin Monster"
behind wooden bars.
Never mind the ugliness,
there's love in his obsession.

Look at me quietly, closely,
a man turned 60.
See how the light confirms
the mask of age: my hair
still black as crow, no wrinkles,
no gait peculiar, arthritic.
History can repeat itself.

mermaid

If I have left the land
   to become a fish
you'll find some logic
   in my dream.

Born fifty yards
   from the Indian shoreline
my crib was the sea
   in jak-wood.
The ocean's moon-wailing,
   percussive rolling,
cry of gull,
   the creak of catamarans
straining against the reef
   were all mine,
sounds still zinging
   in my ears.

So water becomes me.
   No thorns to blood my skin,
no flowers to hold my joy
   then suddenly fade to pain;
with dorsal fin
   I'll navigate the sea lanes
swirling by coral pillars,
   water flowers scenting
my silver belly, the polyps
   growing silently with their dreams.

I can now plumb the depths,
   sleep where the stingray sweeps,
come up for sunlight, sweet air,
   to hold my liquid dream.
There's joy in the minnows
   saluting me on their way,

no blood on my gills,
    no sound of feral gasping.

  unless those brined fishermen
    choose once more
  to dip their abattoir hands
    in the sea.

all I ask is my life

Be still. Let this be
the moment for silence.
Speak only with your eyes,
your hair tumbled, your head
tilted in the language of love.
All I ask is my life,

before I suffer again
the old Delta 88's cough and start,
the money-changers at the Royal Bank
with their small talk
and polite computer eyes.

The inner voice
(resolving yesterday's arguments)
drumming advice:
kill the arrogant son-of-a-bitch,
write the blood-and-guts poem,
flee the Arcadian fields,
learn silence
from the raven's rant,

before the piercing drone,
like dust sucking the vacuum's mouth,
the leaden wail that typist girls
fashion in their sweet patience.

If all is noise, decibel hammers,
this old body will tilt, collapse
on its ears—
one moment of silence,
and we have

the necessary atom, life in
equilibrium.

reincarnation

One by one
the kitchen flies would fall
to the swatter's slap,
but not without
the skin on this quiet, gentle man's face
tightening like a drum,
his eyes collecting blood.

Many had seen
the master at work. How his fly-swatter
would come down like lightning,
kill clean as a guillotine.

The trick, he claimed, was to ensure
good kitchen lighting,
a fever in the brain,
the steady nerve of the pyromaniac.

After each performance,
the metempsychosis man
was known to chuckle:
all his flies were bull's eye,
very dead,

all his enemies flat as paper.

some thoughts on the Indian Rope Trick

Even Houdini never set the world on fire
like the legend
of the Indian Rope Trick,
where a basket opens its rattan mouth,
a head of rope springs erect,

surges upward a good twenty feet
and an Indian boy
in a white turban and dhoti
climbs the rope, as if
it were a coconut tree.

The guru of magic
then snaps his black fingers
and boy and rope disappear
into the sweaty air.
No one has ever really seen it happen,
No one has yet broken its magic code.

But watch the Indian snake-charmer compete
as he squats in the pelting sun, lures
his dancing cobra
out of its rattan basket.

How the jewelled head
moves liquid
against the flute's shrill music,
the snake's length of body
always within
that charmed circle of smell
it knows so well.

No poison here to spurt,
no limp bodies to revive
or bury,

only the magic
of the charmer's immunity,
the cobra's virtuoso performance,
classical Kathakali
in animal skin.

elegy for the perfect man

Somewhere in the green hills
    a mansion stews
under an extravagant sun.
    A BENZ pulls out of the driveway.
You're in a Botany 500 suit,
    a red rose in your lapel.
Your beautiful wife seems almost slumped
    in the back seat
heavy with jewels and OBSESSION.
    Do you know
where the wind is churning with hate,
    which eyes are seeking
the Achilles heel ?

So this is the preemptive hour.
    Throw them a sop
to blunt your Croesus face.
    Show them the ooze in your skin
(too many devilled prawns
and dry martinis)
    How your neck bones crack
each time you turn your head,
    those exploding headaches
that follow each business pow-wow.
    Let them in on the true figures
of your mortgage, how you also carry
    the occasional hole
in your silk socks.

This beast always strips
    to the bone.
So trade your BENZ for a LADA,
    your Botany 500 and Italian shoes
for blue jeans and sneakers.
    Only then will the kingdom of love
stretch out its forgiving hands,
    and the perfect man
meet the loving embrace
    for his falling.
Often, there'll be a waiting, a waiting
    for the final spasm
for someone to sip his beer,
    look over the privet fence and say:

    He was too much, too much,
    after all.

legend of the ice-hole child

After yet another convulsive sneeze,
and the wind combing back
his flotsam white hair,
the old storyteller continues:

That's when Angelo, the popsicle man,
toots his horn,
invades the hopscotch bases
with his cold blue pieces of heaven
in his red and white cart.

And all the village children
break rank, swoop down
urgent as locusts;
all, but one
(the one once fished out of an ice hole)
whose eyes are still cold lances,
voice, a frayed and tattered rag .

Please, old man, stop–
don't chase away
my frozen imps and demons
like some Hound of Heaven .
I'll always trade popsicle and laughter
for those dark silences,
secret metaphors
that like gods
stood by the ice hole of my birth.

In the end they say,
a man
grown from the ice-hole child,
squats by the rim of his beginning
and dreams, asking:
what larynx of sun,

legacy of words,
fires this Methuselah man,

storyteller
whose eyeballs seem to laugh,
hands dance as if to Kandyan drums,
whose voice drops silences like thunder
then croons, then rises
to a monsoon scream?

To find out
he breaks him open
from skull bone to crotch.
A hot blood spurts,
and inside

a deep green valley

where the paddy birds
are still whistling in the grass,
coupling and dying fluffed under the sun,
children with candy
on their morning faces
are jumping the hopscotch bases
and Angelo, the popsicle man
is still pushing heaven
in his red and white cart.

breaking the silence

He would sit there
and just look at you.
No thrusting eyes, nothing
unusual about his face,
his body a lump. It was as if
the mediocre flesh
was crowding your eyes like smoke.

But what really nipped
at the heels, drew blood,
smoked up his mother's heart,
was his silence,

a childhood kingdom
forged in some silent vocabulary,
a power unknown, unused;
words in his small mouth locked,
precious as gold? or,
snaked like cobra?

Then one day
he broke his silence
like a sudden rain,
and we like little children
crowded round
his merry-go-round of words,
some bitter and sweet as poetry.

the man who didn't jump from the Golden Gate Bridge

His head, now heavy as cement,
he leans over the bridge,
and asks for something
from the waters below.

And the waters hissing,
whipped by dark shadows, currents
tugging its brown limbs,
protest: not now, not now.

Count the cumulus clouds,
they are too many, too close.
Blue is the colour of death, right only
when the sun flaunts its kingdom
like a peacock.

Only when sunlight embraces my skin,
and I'm running smooth with shimmer,
when the cry of the gull
is joy leaping from its throat.

Don't jump in the shrouded moment
when jumping loses its style,
its tragic architecture, is ugly
like a hurricaned avenue,
an athlete with humps on his back.

If you must jump, jump
in the blue of happiness,
joy shaking hands with death
on a golden day.

the Bilian Tree

Lord, the Bilian Tree
once leaped into my eyes
from some botanical dictionary.
Ever since, it keeps moving in and out,
up and down my mind
like a yo-yo. Why?

It flashed again yesterday
as the sun quivered with blood
then slipped into the horizon;
last year, when summer brought Mr McIver
down our sidewalk, his Shitzu
raising a thin leg
to my precious European Willow.

Why these images of appearance
and disappearance?
those moments that fashioned vulgarity
out of arrogance, a midget dog
thumbing its penis at my face?
And what's all the ducking and diving,
the lightning sleight of hand?

Lord, I now recall definitions,
twisted shadows, shapes:
the Bilian Tree spread like Batman
against the cinnabar of sun
belongs to the sorcerer,
whose fingers are crooked, black magical,
whose heart is imp, cinema,
Bilial.

No art of symmetry,
no Buddha, Bo-Tree Enlightenment,
no softness suggesting love,

or water dancing over pebbles,

only a wood hard as nails,
where no beetle, silverfish
has ever passed through
the corridors of her flesh,
is stubborn, unforgiving,
blood for ever smudging
the woodsman's hands like a curse.

karma

With one rowdy stroke winter
closed autumn's lingering song,

and I said to myself
there's one sure way
to change it all:
give my head

to the stylist
and ask for a make-over
to the free
sixties flower child

with that Jesus look,
sideburns gone wild,
gold earrings   hanging
like fruit from my ears.

Nothing.

The winters rage on,
am still writing poetry.

3

when the raven talks
listen
it is God
in ultimate disguise

return of the fishermen

Dusk. Seagulls grown black
    swoop the catamarans
pitching their prows homeward.
    Tired bodies arch,
hug the lifeline of ropes,
    home now urgent
in their blood, closer
    to their black creviced faces.

Sea-stained eyes
    comb the beach
for the relics they left behind:
    fat and scowling women,
children   naked
    with bulging bellies,
pariah dogs barking
    at the breaking waves.

They disgorge their catch
    at the feet
of a short fat mudalali.
    He had bought their catch
and their souls long ago.

But for now,
    it is Seer fish in the pan,
coconut toddy, mango breasts bare
    on their wives.
Children cling and cry,
    dogs scratch and whine,
bodies ache, rice boils

and the sea throbs on.

And men and dogs,
    toddied women and children
soon fall to wearied sleep.
    There is peace in the sun,
in the palm-thatched huts
    of the fishermen.

Only the sea throbs on.

he who talks to the raven

talks to God,
    black-feathered and beaked
with toe nails growing inward,
    a mouth full of caw.
Superb surveyor of the skies,
    postman to history
happening by the second,
    foul-mouthed, he sings
the sweetest song, black-eyed
    he outdoes the morning sun.

He who talks to the raven
    shares parables,
some windows of possibility:
    if the water's at the bottom
of the pitcher,
    throw pebble after pebble
and the level will rise like bread
    to the top.
If the desert churns your thirst
    know that there's water
breeding in the cactus.

He who talks to the raven
    talks to the bird humming

with ESP in its brain:
> who knows the distant agony
of the goat even as the anaconda
> unhinges its jaws;
the byways of the eagle's ether flight
> before it traps
the rabbit's frozen eyes.

He who talks to the raven
> long enough, learns
how the sweet wood apple
> disappears in the elephant's mouth,
how to say: caw   caw   caw
> when the gongs of hunger
ring like church bells.
> How when something lurches,
is ready to strike,
> can suddenly stride
into the face of the sun,
> keep the rose between his teeth
and say: caw   caw   caw.

This bird is bore
> and diplomat
will take your gifts
> and demand for more, insist
that you understand its importunate ways,
> love it, stroke its velvet wing.

When the raven talks,
> listen,
it is God
> in ultimate disguise.

waif

The Indian Sea's blue rollers,
hem of blonde beach
and I am seduced once more.
Again the architect to the sand castles,
ragamuffin stoning the sand crabs,
plucking seaweed
from their liquid dance,

when I hear a child cry.
Naked, alone   his back to the sea,
under hunting gulls, he is crying
and crying and crying.
I try the language of a child,
ask him why,
then recall bamboo kites and ice cream
on the Galle Face Green,
but the child wails
and the sea wails.
Again, I beg for reasons.
Nothing. Only his spouting eyes,
the muffled drums of the sea.

I then cry too, become
another lost child, wet sand
under my feet,
sea and gull nagging my ears.
Suddenly   he stops crying,
stretches out a trembling hand,
his eyes   for home . . .

the outlaw and the orchid

Sardiel's mountain cave,
bare as bones and fiercely cold,

is not without decor:
a single orchid explodes the darkness.

Petalled skin like fevered salmon,
it's an upside-down Grecian goblet

that bares violet inside a chaliced throat,
breathes over straw mat, sleeping gun,

a dagger catching the pale flicker of an oil lamp.
Legs, in lotus mode, the vagabond

is chewing his betel leaf like a goat.
He rises. Sidles up to his exotic flower,

spits the blood-red betel juice
into its velvet throat.

Lies down. Arranges his thin black hands for pillow,
falls   into fitful sleep.

The orchid still spills its shapely effulgence.
The outlaw collects the new blood into his dreams.

Kukul Charlie

The circle widens.
    Half-naked street urchins,
    a woman with a child in arms,
    an old man, a Buddhist monk
    close in, strain their ears to catch
    each nuance of sound, seeking
    the flaw, the imperfect note
    from the man
    who claimed the voice of animals.

First, the midnight ritual
    of two fighting alley cats.
    Body language and decibels
    ride in perfect unison,
    the crowd numbs into silence.
    If KUKUL (Chicken) Charlie
    was his name,
    then the sounds of chickens
    were right up there
    in his repertoire.

Here's the hen's cry of triumph
    after the ceremony of eggs,
    here's the rooster
    with head high up in the air,
    comb titillating in the sun,
    circling the chosen one,
    its courting voice perfect
    in Charlie's throat.
    And how does the peacock cry
    just before the breaking rain?
    Charlie arches his thin body,
    straightens up with a jerk,
    lets out that eerie cry
    like some invention of hell.

His tin cup sings
    to the metallic throw of coins,
    the crowd is putty in his hands.
But one last act–the cry
of a baby with a colic
and a sudden doubt
invades the once admiring faces.
His audience slips,
is fast unravelling.
The woman with babe in arms
shouts in anger: Go home, you animal,
and listen to your own children cry!

4

holding Heaven in a waterbead

the accepted one

For relics
        a black soutane
bronze cross
        lying limp
on a breviary
        bloodied
with the martyrdom
        of celibacy

They found
        the cathedral of his cloister
empty
    Pray my brothers they cried
he now walks the earth
        without
surplice and soul

Fr Magee opened
        a door
to the old cabook house
                a woman
and no icons

And God
        did not pitch the sun
with dark thoughts

heart of the matter

Where a door opens
   to the mood
   of your half-naked body,
   your knuckles still growing blue,
   a trace of blood
   round your mouth. Civilization
   with knuckle dusters on its fists.

Where a woman bends
   over a cradle,
   rocks it gently.
   And her song, her kingdom,
   is a lullaby in the air,
   her infant soon falling to sleep.

Where the reading lamp's yellow light
   picks out the still fierce eyes
   of an old man, a poem of hope:
   "Still falls the rain."
   Lightning round an ancient cross
   he has already seen, waiting
   for cock's crow and laughter.

Where the maid
   to this house of small rooms
   deserts her mop and crumpled beds,
   irreverent corners of dirt
   and stumbles into Thomas A Kempis
   all dressed up in sack cloth and ashes
   holding Heaven in a waterbead, singing:

   "Vanity of vanities,
   all is vanity
   save to love God
   and Him only to serve."

" Yes, in our Father's House there are many rooms "

Lord, say: Come,
    I have a place for you here.
I'd like to hear the magic words
    from your Almighty Mouth,
and please, no archangel,
    Burning Bush, sudden revelation
by the broken ankles of a fallen horse.

It's time, Lord, to redeem a promise.
    Your Blessed Mother once assured me
of the Kingdom of Heaven
    if I became a Rosary Nut!
I did, and still recall the night
    I heard the wind bawl out
like a baby,

the apple tree by my window
    convulse in pain,
some hand clamp shut
    the gates of hell,
the night I found my peace
    on earth.

I'm sure she understood my pain,
    saw how my face grew dark as beet
as mocking words found their target:
    "Here he comes, fat rosary wimp"
or, "There he goes, Mr Santa Maria Rosary Man "

hobo who never knew
    the polished touch of mother-of-pearl,
only cheap coloured glass,
    beads with crooked crosses
all so entangled
    that no fingers could quite unravel

these holy knots.

So here I come, O Lord,
    but before St Peter
stamps my passport
    may I ask a few mundane favours?
I'd like my room to be a replica
    of my master bedroom
at 166, McGregor Cres. Waterloo;

A colour TV would be nice
    (preferably a 24 inch)
would help to look in on Columbo,
    Cosby and Matlock,
keep track of what's happening
    in "The Heat of the Night."
I almost forgot,
    I'd also like to beg
for some spaces
    for my kids and my good wife, Anne.
So could you please
    change the accommodation
to a small bungalow?

I was also thinking
    (if you don't mind)
of bringing along
    my ten books of poetry,
some copies of the "Elegies" I wrote
    for my dad, my ma,
and my brother, Hilary.

I guess, Lord,
    all this might seem
very strange to you,
    but then again not at all.
I know something about
    the Vision of God,
the metaphysical state,

    space without space, time
with no name, legend or end,

but remember?
    I'm right now only in the prison
of my own shapes, the heart,
    the eyes still holding on
to thin glass, seeing
    and not seeing,

the flesh still breathing,
    heaving, the blood as the river
flowing on, and yet
    I wait for your call,
that Heaven once promised
    in the small blue beads
of my broken rosary.

5

    ... separate
in its greenness, a stone
contradicting stone ...

how an old poet beat loneliness to death

When a solstice sun
flaps its ears
and rubs its red nose
on the window pane,
his children gather up
their small rambuttan heads,
voices, itchy summer feet
and run outdoors,

leaving an old man
in his room
with lead balls hanging
from the root of his tongue,
a strip of Sahara growing
under his fragile ribs.

Loneliness, however,
is but a poem unborn.
So the old man gathers
    a stone,
    a clump of grass,
    three glass marbles
    and a dead sparrow
and lays them beside him
on the carpet floor.

The stone
        breathes,
stutters and stammers,
green blades
        leap the marimba,
the dead bird
        throbs,
arches and opens
its stunned eyes

to a smiling old man
with a poem in his hand.

poetics

Like an animal
the word
hunts the poet,
paralyses him (to other choices);
or, the poet, the word ?

in either case,
there is a killing
and a resurrection,
like the Digger Wasp
that paralyses the spider,
lays a single egg
in its belly,
and waits patiently
for its sweet wasp.

letter of thanks to my first creative writing teacher

for Michael Estok

You pose on the back cover
of *Paradise Garage*
with the abandon of a banian,
a summer casualness
suggesting a pure joy of the sun;
a young Keats, perhaps,
after too much of cheap wine.

I've read the poems very carefully:
    Chansons Acadiennes
    Spells and Curses
    Desperate Solidarities–
all lean and muscled like stallions,
nowhere near my fat sun, my hefty words,
my wounds red as shoe flowers.

You sing nothing but the polished stone,
the exact chirrup of a dying cricket,
the subtle magic in the prairie fire,
the kernel, the kernel,
husk and shell out on the rubbish heap.

I broke all the rules–
how can the sun chatter in my teeth,
the snow make a sweet warm fire
under my feet,
the body and brain listen
to the mad and searing disorder of words?

When I coloured, I coloured wildly,
feather of Ibis, the sun
with blood on its face.
When I killed, I mauled clumsily,

could never shoot clean between the eyes.

So what of my poetry?
My madness? my dancing on the edge,
my exotic metaphors, my falling?
Was there something in the books,
the way I hammered out my song,
the wound's percussion?

No? You perhaps heard
those rare silences of my thunder,
noted my quiet bravado, that art
of crashing the snow fences
for a patch of kingdom in the sun.

So welcome, my friend,
to the Published Poets' Club.
I'd leave Buriyani Rice and Prawn Curry
to the poetics of the Sun-Man,
they'll never sit right or ever zing
in your poems.
And Sir, hang on to your Rye Whisky,
the Sri Lankan Arrack
scars the throat, burns,
burns like nothing else on earth.

the separate one

Look carefully
at this stone.
Once ribbed to a cold black mound
it is now   alone separate
in its greenness, a stone
contradicting stone,
a throat full of honey,
an argument of moss,
a kingdom of distilled water.

Much like the man
I once knew–
going mad with the crowd
in one direction
was never his style.
So he danced a solo, chose
his own idiom of madness.

How he smelled the herd,
read the wind, rituals
of pounding hooves, ribcage to ribcage,
the way their eyes
butted each other, body heat
churned their thirst.

Alone, he would have the river's edge,
shade of Acacia, a horizon of eagle
against the sun.
He could now laugh or cry, bellow
if he must,
and the poem would follow him
like a faithful dog.

6

**our passion for the happy story
that would never end**

domestic history

Say, 50 years ago:
another sun, another sky,
another colour the earth–
and housework moved
with the rhythm
of a metronome.

My mother up at 4:00,
or latest by cock's crow,
the house soon sunning
on love and small warm hands:
milk-rice and curry, hot tea,
bananas, the breakfast spread
smiling into our sleepy faces.

My sisters made my bed,
picked up my bermuda shorts, gauze banians
smelling of yesterday's sweat;
my marbles, tramcar tickets
strewn like confetti all over the floor;
a coconut-fibre broom
quietly covered every other sin
my room had to offer.

I now drive an OLDS 98, Regency Brougham,
savour its luxury like a lollipop.
My home cradles among manicured lawns,
Japanese Maple, European Willow, catalpa,
LINCOLN and Riviera often showing
their elegant faces down the street.

So why am I hauling this vacuum
up the stairs with a mild grimace,
why the curses flooding

my closed mouth?
And why do I put up with the scarring noise
of this sucking machine ?

I'm standing by the sink
(thinking of my dear mother,
my sisters, my token money of tram tickets)
as the load of dirty dishes
squirming and fuming
gnash their teeth and ask:
what the hell are you waiting for?

love poem for Anne # 2

Having done the chocolate cake,
    patis and candy trays,
    you are moon-huddled
    under a passing cloud,
    the kitchen chair holding your sleep
    like china:

Our bodies laid out, limp
    under the champagne sun,
    when a butterfly in sweet chartreuse
    tags your braided hair,
    then seduces me
    with her flirting dance
    across the mango groves.

I leave you behind
    to write the poem, you
    who never understood the stars
    in my brain, the dark image of fire,
    who once saw the eagle's geometry
    in the sky
    as no different from the tumble
    of the raven,

is now the suicide moth
    tangoing with the flame,
    and I, your lover poet,
    taken in by summer's filigree,
    heady under the sweet mango air,
    am chasing this yellow bauble of wings.

So here's to you, my love,
    for shucking the oyster of your dream,
    opening out the pearl,
    the precious poetry.

genetics

The fire
    that is fire
    that must burn
    tomorrow and tomorrow
bares the face
    a name, a gait,
    that makes you heir
    to this kingdom
    of flesh and blood.

So the story is told
    retold,
    how from behind, my son,
    the view
    is your father's hunch,
    brief neck,
    that lumbering gait,
    the nape thick and brown
    as jaggery.

Your mother jokes
    at this logic
    of imperfections,
    I, proud
    as a fixed star,
    of the inexorable fire,
    genetics
    that sees nothing
    but my own face,
    even your childish babble
    sheer poetry.

elegy for an elder brother

After your death, Hilary,
I saw you flash by in riding clothes,
a whip singing in the air,
boots catching the fire
of the sun.
Hunting? for what?
No quarry, no guns, no dogs,
only cloud and rain
about your ears,

and then I remembered,
I knew: the way
you held your eyes to Heaven,
ran your thin black fingers
over your scientific head
as the runnels of the heart
smoked and clogged
and you muttering the tried mantarams
of your life: Deus, Deus,
O Mother of God,
Thomas, my Doctor Angelicus,
Augustine, beloved sinner and saint,
Hopkins, Merton, Teilhard,
my wounded country, my Decima,
my dear ones . . .

Be still O Hound of Heaven,
the helminthologist, the philosopher,
is dead!
The worm, he always said, belongs to God,
is God,
his sweet obsession, his Ph D piece
of candy, his metaphor for the good earth,
his perfect passport
to the Academy of Academies.

the perfect hobbyist

for Michael

His five-year-old legs
    take the long hours by the aquarium
    like an elephant happy
    under an Acacia tree.
    His black eyes forever trained
    on the clear sea-green water.

Our hobbyist can now identify
    black molly or platy,
    separate the guppies from the zebras,
    mimic the "o" of the goldfish's mouth,
    even claim that the rasboras
    surface for air at his call.
    The apprenticeship seems over,
    until

He takes one small step
    from looking to doing,
    one huge step for boyhood–
    and a whole tin of fish food
    is cast over the waters,
    and nothing but a thick white powder
    seals the stomachs, the lives
    of all living creatures
    wiggling under his eyes.

And God laughs,
    breaking the matted clouds
    into shimmering rain

and I, hammering words
    into a small boy's frightened face,
    forget

my own green and foolish days,
the fantastic limits
of his generosity,
his compassion for the hungry
sweeter than kitul honey,
his superb madness
for trying to be
the perfect hobbyist.

for Michael dancing with his hands on his head

Michael, this is heavy stuff
I'm listening to, the London Philharmonic
playing Beethoven's Ninth.
It hardly suggests gyrations
with the hands on the head.

Some advice, just in case
this spinning world has got you
like the Bogey Man–
Do not decide to jump off.
First try ducking, leaning, surging,
praying, fighting, T.M., loving.
If all these strategies fail,
try walking backwards,
or spinning counter-clockwise–
It's called de-sensitization.
After all that spinning,
you won't know
who's spinning whom.

So, carry on son, dancing
with your hands on your head.
In Ceylon, some used to call this dance
the Devil's Dance, others
the Buddhu-Amme Dance, meaning
"O my God" dance.

love poem for Anne #3

This poem
is for those
>who cannot read
>the cry of the raven,
>who watch a monsoon rain
>and still don't know the raindrop.

For those
>for whom the sun is without love,
>only a torch of slow pain;
>who swear under their breath
>as they trample the first snows,
>will not warm
>a lost snowflake in their palms.

For those
>who cannot take
>a baby's urgent cry,
>refuse the language of its gurgle;
>who look into an old man's eyes
>and see nothing
>but death curdling in his veins.

For those
>without ears for angelus bells,
>without heart
>for the saffron robe and begging bowl;
>who walk their dogs at night,
>are blind to the boulevard's living dead,
>their monuments veiled in dung.

For those
>who cannot see another Christ
>in the wino
>seduced by his bottle,

        the dark fog of his alley.

This poem
        is for you
        who from the beginning
        taught me
        the way of flowers.

leaving –Michael style

These are the fractured journeys
of childhood
where the hairline crack
seems wider than a chasm;
where we learn
the true nylon toughness
of the umbilical cord,
how to love
what we think we hate
in the terror of argument,
hate what we know
is not our mother,
only the genius
of a child's topsy-turvy room,
a set of rioting loafing toys.

So a hectoring voice
once again lays out the charges:
Michael, toys all over the damn place
and they're going
straight into the garbage!

Batman in the dumpster?
Tears drown out the thought.
He makes the traumatic decision.
He must leave . . .

Says so defiantly: I'm leaving!
And mum, cool as tea-country rain,
picks up the gauntlet :
Good. Let me pack your bags!

A sheet of paper
is left behind revealing
a superb map
of his " leaving" itinerary,
his last stop, a legend
that seemed washed ashore
by the tides of the womb:
I WILL BE FOUND HERE!

The anchors hold.
Congenital love survives
the deep frost
as the fires of dissent burn out
by the map's end.
This is a going, a kind of love
that always leaves a paper trail,
that never goes out at all.

connections of a passionate sort

for Deena

You only two days old
and we let the photographer
shadow your crib, flash
his delicate machinery like lightning.
How else to mirror ourselves,
fashion our clones,
feed our genetic urge
for history, documentation,
our passion for the happy story
that would never end.

Photographs,
all arranged and paid for
by us who are caught up
in King Kong's hairy arms
for that involuntary journey
into the shadowed musty castle
where our lives, photos
silently gather the blurring mould
of memory   but you
my Viking daughter still softening
the mercurial pain
of growing old.

a time for epitaphs

for Deena

Winter's gone
    and Pablo, the snow blower,
is now a quiet shining lump
    in the corner of the garage.
The sun deck bares its claw marks,
    raw wood showing up in places
like wounds.

Again the crocus
    looking anonymous as ever
and yet raking memory
    (those seductive surprises
of my first spring)
    setting up the future
like a stage. In the end,
    whatever raps the gnarled ice,
pries carbuncles
    with so much style
deserves some applause.

Summer. The Maple leaps to green,
    a child's giggling laughter
rides like birthday balloons
    in the hot air,
The freezer scowls
    as the tomatoes jostle for position.
Children are back,
    their husbands, tiny clones.
Deena is silently wrecking
    my arctic carpet,
granddaughter immunity
    all over her grinning face.

And there goes
    the coffee table's prize trophy,
the Kandyan Dancer
    now without an arm and a leg.
Summer seems to be going
    under another name: pandemonium.
So why am I talking
    of seasons gone, come
to the prologue of autumn
    for that exotic undressing,
that time for the leaf's long sleep.

I can almost see the epilogue,
    my own.
Anne is shuffling
    round the kitchen table,
a song loud in her head, home
    her one metaphor for love.
Michael, super architect at 10,
    is Michael, a loud rhetoric
in his mouth,
    some ants in his pants.
John keeps his precious silences,
    writes his own music
lives his metaphysical poem.

And I'm beginning
    to hear voices, warnings,
feel as if the warm blonde light
    is holding God like a presence:

    this is your harvest, my man,
    take it, take it with both hands,
    savour the prism of its ways
    as would an infant its disney mobile,

    time is written on desert sand.

What now?
    Has the time for epitaphs
finally come?
    What words will fire like lightning
those filaments of a man's life and death?
    What legends will crowd my gravestone?
Wish I could write my own epitaph
    without the cold truth,
doing only the poetic thing
    with the profound and passionate lie.

sunday morning

Separate sounds,
church bells and bullets
intersect in the same man;
a black harbinger dog
limps across the Sunday sky.

The old wino's bottle
cries in its dregs,
alley walls soak in his pain,
the wet stones
silently smudge a new grave,
and bodies in Sunday clothes
are slowly moving their limbs to pray.

The sun
without discrimination
warms the forgotten pulse,
the black smoking head,
Christ slumped against a garbage can,

and Sunday clothes
are slowly moving their bodies to pray.